The King's Comeuppance

By

Robert Selby

Co-authored by

Iris Patton

E-Book ISBN: 979-8-89397-920-6

Paperback ISBN: 979-8-89397-921-3

Hardcover ISBN: 979-8-89397-922-0

Disclaimer

This work contains characters and events that are intentionally inspired by real people and circumstances; however, all portrayals have been adapted for narrative purposes, and creative liberties have been taken to shape the story's fictional framework. These representations should not be interpreted as exact depictions of any individual's actions, views, or experiences. The author expresses sincere appreciation to the Trump family for their influence and the inspiration they provided during the creative process.

Dedication

Dedicated to my children, Marcie, Nick, and April, with all my love.

Foreword

When I first met Robert, I had no idea that an unlikely little friendship was beginning to form. Yet here we are, something simple, genuine, and unexpectedly meaningful, and it feels like such a gift to be able to introduce his work.

The King's Comeuppance is more than a story. It's a window into Robert's imagination, his sincerity, and the quiet passion he pours into every line. Reading this book, you can feel his heart woven through the pages, the tenderness, the creativity, the cinematic sweep of the story, and the steady warmth underneath it all.

Watching a friend turn an idea into a finished book is a beautifully special thing. I'm so proud of him for bringing this tale to life, and even prouder to stand here, at the front of it, sharing in his achievement. This story carries adventure, emotion, and a unique charm that makes you want to linger in its world just a little longer.

It's an honor to write this foreword, and an honor to know the person behind these pages. I hope you enjoy this book as much as I have, and that you feel the same heart, care, and devotion that went into every word.

- Draci Lynne Farmer
American ventriloquist and singer

Preface

This story, starring the president's grand-daughter, was written over a decade ago, just prior to him announcing his decision to run for the WH. One of his first stumps was at the Factory, in Franklin, TN. And I decided I would let fate decide if I would write the last chapter, by going to that speaking engagement with a note written on the back of a business card.

To wit, I've penned a story and your grand-daughter is the main character. I stood outside the Factory building, with a couple of hundred people that couldn't fit inside, in the misty rain, listening to him talk, inside, about his favorite person. It seemed a futile endeavor, until he finished and exited out a door not a dozen feet from where I stood. He waded into the crowd, right up to me, broadcasting as he walked. When he stopped in front of me, I handed him my prepared card. He turned and slowly walked a few steps toward his black suburban, while reading my note. Then stopped, turned around facing me, made eye contact, smiled and gave me a thumbs up.

Then jumped into his car and was gone. Leaving me thinking.

Now, I "have" to finish the story. That was a decade ago.

Recently a young woman, quite skilled with words, reached out to me, and convinced me to let her shape and finish the story. The following is that tale, and the opinions and insights of those reading about BB and her exceptional life, will influence fate going forward. Happy trails…

About the Author

About the writer, this story was recorded prior to DT expressing his intent to run for office. It was put on hold after he was elected for a plethora of reasons, the biggest being avoiding becoming a target. The primary reason for its conception was adding a physicality aspect to golf, the centuries-old sport that's popular worldwide, but always considered a sport lacking in physical demands. I bought a trike and converted it to a golf cart with a goal in mind. Some courses wouldn't allow it, but most did. The interest from other golfers was exceptional, and the workout it added was at times more than I had in me. Adding a seductive aspect to a sport I've loved since childhood is a mission of passion to improve and make more alluring the sport of golf, for the youngest generation, and all who love playing.

I'm completing another book regarding the subject of clean energy. Over the last eight years, I've designed and tested an innovative hydro technology that offers to produce more clean energy, electrical, and green hydrogen than the world can use; Produced substantially less expensively than any present source. The most compelling aspect regarding these dam-less waterway systems, employing WCM, is their mobility to be moved to best serving locations, and that units can be assembled within months vs decades for many sources. Over 100 units could be assembled for the cost of one new nuclear facility. Each unit produces the equivalent output of that one landlocked source. This tech holds the key to pushing the transition into the Electrical Era within this decade. Collaboration is underway between TVA and ORNL to perform a large-scale test to match data produced against the calculations offered by AI. My book relating the eight-year, ongoing journey should be out in early 2026. Thanks.

Prologue

It had been about half an hour and we were still moving. It seemed surreal that we had actually made it even the first sixty seconds, though we always thought that the downside was quite minimal, at least in the first few minutes. Now that we were away from the crowd it was becoming more apparent by the minute that the first twenty-four hours would be the make or break for our, or rather, *my*, breakout.

The tournament was finished, in fact, the entire last three days were long forgotten altogether. All that mattered, and what engaged my psyche, was staying ahead of the growing force being employed to stop our getaway. I had to put those thoughts aside and concentrate on the moment at hand, the decisions that kept us ahead of our hunters.

Less than an hour ago, I was teeing off on eighteen with a pretty comfortable lead, and determined to close out a record setting round. Though even I was surprised with *the* chip-in eagle on the closing hole to record the lowest round of this major event; and aware that my time was as good or better than my previous personal best. All of that was quickly forgotten when we put the plan into action and walked out the club house door with my heart pounding in my chest. I knew the first five seconds were critical. If the secret service agents recognized us then our plan would have unraveled before it even started.

Yet here we were, trading our original means of escape for a nondescript RV, and so far, we were still somehow moving. Isn't love grand? And freedom… a word that never meant as much to me as it does presently. Freeing myself from eighteen years of scrutiny had become my ever present dream, but it never seemed more than a dream until now.

Before this very moment it had all only been escape plans and *what ifs* and *what-can-we-how-can-we*s, but now the more distance we covered, the longer we stayed on the road, the more real it became.

No longer a dream. No longer a wish, a prayer, a hope. But more of a present moment they were living in. And despite all the preparation and planning and thought put into it, no one could've prepared them for the overwhelming wave of feelings that threatened to take over. The anticipation of what was going to happen next. The anxiety of failing and getting caught. The determination of not wanting to let it happen.

His grip tightened on the wheel, and only one thought rang through: *failure was not an option.*

Table of Contents

Chapter 1: The Plan in Motion

Forty Minutes Ago

The anticipation was driving me crazy and I guess that was a factor in how well I played and timed in the last round. When I got to the tee on the last par 5 finishing hole, my whole body was shaking, perhaps humming is a better word. And not because of how effortlessly the previous seventeen holes had disappeared, but because of the plan we had made. It had never seemed quite real until I was floating down the eighteenth fairway chasing my drive. The thought that in literally minutes I might be starting a new life, a major change from my previous one.

Minutes before I'd have to say goodbye to everything I've known and have been familiar with my whole life, whether that was in good faith or contempt. I've found that goodbyes were never black or white as people made them seem to be. A beginning of a new life of a new adventure always brought along with it the bitterness and even grief of the end of the previous one.

Everything was going to change.

I thought about the man waiting for me to share our plan — or rather I should say, my plan, which he had so graciously encouraged, supported, and was as determined as I to carry out. In fact, he had been the one to surreptitiously position all the accoutrements necessary for our plan to succeed while I competed in the tournament. The highly touted international major *Trike-Golf* tournament was the perfect cover for our planned escape. As daring as it sounded, it felt like the best distraction imaginable.

A few minutes after completing my round — to near-deafening applause all the way down eighteen, particularly when my ball rolled into the cup for an eagle — I walked out of the scorer's tent and into the women's locker room. Arrangements had been made in advance for me to use the locker room for a brief post-tournament interview while the trophy ceremony details were finalized. We believed those few minutes would be our best opportunity to slip away before anyone realized I had vanished.

The setup involved my soon-to-be companion creating the interview scene in the game room of the women's locker room — the only room with a door leading outside. An agent had been stationed at that door to guard the "interview room" and prevent anyone from entering — a crucial part of our subterfuge. We had hired an assistant of my same shape and height, with long, flaming red hair, and a cameraman matching his build and appearance. They were instructed to enter through that specific outside door after being thoroughly vetted by the agent. Each wore coveralls and golf caps that matched those of the club's support staff uniforms complete with the same logo and *"Staff"* printed across the back. Oversized, distinctive sunglasses added the final touch to *our* ultimate disguise.

As I walked from the scorer's tent into the women's locker room, two female agents with hand mics were already inside. I asked them not to allow anyone access to the interview room during the taping, then entered and closed the door behind me. Across the room, the outside door was being held open by the agent for the assistant and cameraman to enter. Once both doors were shut, the support crew was asked to set their caps and glasses on the table and wait in the main locker room for a couple of minutes while I reviewed the particulars of the interview.

As soon as the door closed behind them, I gave the same message to the agents — that they would be needed in a couple of minutes, — and matching coveralls and a red-haired wig were produced. We quickly dressed for our parts, and proceeded to the outside door.

Adrenaline surged through my body as we stepped out. It was nerve wrecking. My partner in crime informed the agent that we, the crew members, would be re-entering in a few minutes after interview specifics were addressed inside the game room. We went straight to the electric golf cart provided to the crew by the club and drove off.

The odds were highest against us at that moment. Our plan was in full swing, and we were heading toward freedom — never once looking back. The only way forward was through. Those first few seconds felt like hours as we reached the parking lot and the vehicle we had previously parked according to plan.

Split-second timing was essential as we traded our cart for another identical to the tournament's staff carts — this one re-engineered with a far more powerful engine so it could aid us in getting away far quicker than an average golf cart. It also assured us that anyone else who tried to follow us in their carts would be left behind, unless they decided to ditch the golf vehicles and get their own, which would take far too long. The details of this plan had been fine-tuned carefully over months.

Once inside the cart, I quickly removed the wig, and we exchanged hats and sunglasses before taking the path that led to a bridge spanning the river dividing the course from the bordering estates. Prior to the tournament, one of those homes had been rented under our arrangement as part of the escape plan, and we steered the cart directly into its attached garage.

Waiting for us inside were twin drones, computer-controlled, each large enough to carry our individual weight. We had each practiced separately for weeks, hoping we would never actually need to use them. Fifteen minutes later, we ditched the drones in a barn that concealed our nondescript RV. Now, we were headed for the nearest interstate — the quickest route to put as much distance between us and everything behind us as possible.

In roughly twenty-two minutes, we would be exiting the main road and begin our journey along the backroads that lead to freedom and romance. I'd never felt such unadulterated excitement, fear, and joy altogether squirming inside me into a jumble of feelings that left me weak-kneed and determined at the same time. Constantly chanting to myself to pull through to stay strong and keep going. This was the only chance that we'll get to live our lives according to us, to love and laugh and cry over things that were ours and ours alone.

With this in thought, we set towards our future.

Chapter 2: Secrets and Codes

One Week Ago

The idea and the plan born from it, was quickly coming to hope-filled fruition. For months, we had exchanged texts and emails, refining the details and requisites of our grand scheme. As with the previous three years, since we first met and began a virtual relationship, we had become even more diligent about using coded communication. The outside forces that would undermine our plan if they suspected anything had to remain completely in the dark, as they had been for years. No one could find out before we were ready to reveal it to the people we wanted to. It had to be on our terms, whatever the nature of our secret was or whatever the motivation was behind keeping it, it was for us to know and no one else.

My family and close friends call me Bel or Bella, while most of the world refers to me simply as "B" in relation to my sports and philanthropic work. My family — both immediate and extended — is among the most well-known in this country, and perhaps the world. My parents and grandfather have lived their entire lives in the public spotlight, and so have I. It is the most compelling reason for my desire to escape. I have spent my life under twenty-four-hour scrutiny — by my parents, by government agents, and to a lesser degree by everyone employed by "the family." Now, now that I was able to, I wanted to escape it all and live a normal life, whatever that may have looked like, I was willing to accept it and face it.

Golf — golf courses, tournaments, and the game itself — was the thread that bound our family together. It was also the cornerstone of many of our family's prized assets, particularly those of my grandfather. I have played nearly all of those family-owned courses at one time or another and was good enough that now I found them not as exciting as others around me with similar interests. The only reason I even continued with golfing was because that was all I knew up until now, it was my family's legacy — our dynasty. I could share our names, but that seems both unnecessary and disrespectful, considering the plan we were plotting.

My paramour — through three years of communication — is named Spirodon, after his great-grandfather. His family may be as famous, or infamous, as mine, depending on whom you ask, though they rarely bask in the endless glare of social media, print, and television, the way certain members of my family do. His grandfather is the most well-known of all Russians.

We have never shared a kiss, though we've often talked about how much we long for that first moment. We've hugged a few times, after interviews I've done with him. He is, and has been, one of the very few people to whom I've granted interviews. Publicity has never been an appealing part of my success in the sport that made my name so widely known. Very few journalists respect my intentions, when I agree to speak — the purpose of every interview has always been to promote my passion for helping others, not to fuel vapid notoriety, the kind that seems to follow several members of my family.

Three years ago, Spiro requested an interview and accompanied his proposal with a note that showed he understood my boundaries. I agreed, on the condition that I would walk out if it drifted from my specific goals.

I was fifteen then, and Spiro was nineteen. The moment I met him, it felt as though I had known him forever. From my side, it felt like kismet, though I did my best not to show how deeply he affected me. As it turned out, through our near-daily correspondence after that interview, he confessed that he had felt the same—that he was in a daze through most of that first meeting. When our time together ended, he hugged me goodbye, and I felt tremors run through my body and a light show behind my eyes. It was unnerving and exhilarating at once—and painfully hard to let go. I wanted to hold him forever.

He later wrote the most beautiful piece, one that exceeded all my expectations and reflected my mission perfectly. Afterward, I read many of his works—most needing translation from his Slavic language—and came to admire how deeply his writing connected to his homeland. By then, he already had rock-star status in his country, more for his talent than his lineage.

After that first encounter, we exchanged personal contact information with the promise to stay in touch. Soon, our notes became regular, and I suggested a way to code our messages to elude the ever-present eyes surrounding my life.

He had been respectful of my intentions from the start. It was one of the things that drew me to him in the first place. His attentiveness and intent on listening and respecting the things that I expressed passion about and the way he in turn articulated himself so beautifully showing that he cared enough to be well-versed on the topics, too. Even if we didn't agreed on a thing, his soft smiles that he graced me with, assuring me that I was still important to him, that despite our disagreements, I'll never lose his respect — were enough for me to know that this was a person that I wanted to keep in my life, in what capacity I hadn't decided yet. But soon after, as I got to know him better, as we *both* got to know each other better, I felt my feelings towards him change and grow into something fonder and permanent.

That initial meeting had been pure chance — a coincidence of timing. I was playing in a Trike Golf tournament that happened to coincide with a diplomatic visit between his grandfather and my own. The course, one of my family's properties near Washington, was my stage that weekend. Spiro reached out the day before the final round. It wasn't clear then, but looking back, it seems that destiny had intervened, binding our paths together.

Over the next three years, as our connection blossomed into romance, he continued to pursue his craft, while I competed at the highest levels of national and international tournaments. During those years, he managed to attend two of my events for follow-up interviews. Each time, being in the same room with him felt like stepping into a bubble — where the only people who existed was us and the rest of the world disappeared. The entourage that constantly surrounded me, and the one that followed him when he traveled, seemed to vanish into the background. When we were together, it felt as though the horizon itself faded away.

I would have given anything to kiss him each time he held me in his arms. But we had agreed through our correspondence that we couldn't risk showing any overt affection — nothing that might've invited scrutiny or suspicion. We couldn't afford to create obstacles imposed by our respective overseers, especially mine.

Discretion was always our top priority. Even though all our hearts and souls wanted was to be wrapped in each other's arms and never let go, to show the world how much we meant to each other. But temporary sacrifices had to be made no matter how suffocating it felt in order for us to be free and together in the future.

So, we settled into this routine of familiar strangers that only crossed paths in scheduled times.

Chapter 3: The World Watches

It's been exactly six days, and activity across the United States — and much of the world, particularly in Russia — has been consumed by the disappearance, whereabouts, and well-being of the two most-watched people on the planet. The missing BB and Serg have vanished without a trace. Some calling it a kidnapping, others something worse.

After a week of interrogation and countless repeated questions, the Secret Service has kept me close at hand, though they've learned no more than what I told them from the beginning. And I made sure what they knew was not what would harm us in any capacity.

Apparently, April could offer no more than I could to the first agents who questioned us. A few minutes after I regained consciousness on the floor of the ladies' locker room, the most surreal experience of this already chaotic ordeal unfolded: BB's mother, IV, and her commander-in-chief father, DT, entered the room and discovered that their precious family member was missing.

In the moments that followed their arrival, the atmosphere erupted into chaos. Father and daughter filled the room with a torrent of emotions — from disbelief to rage — and suddenly it was a storm of people, voices, and demands all colliding at once. Within minutes of the American royals entering, April and I were physically escorted by a half-dozen men in suits down the hallway into the bathroom, where the questioning intensified.

Eventually, April and I were separated. I was taken to a van, driven a short distance, and placed in a windowless room. Barely an hour had passed since I had woken to the news of BB's disappearance, and now I sat alone in a small interrogation room.

The most striking memory of those first moments was the fear in the eyes of the two agents assigned to interview me. It was immediately apparent that they were torn between their need to extract every detail and their awareness of my potential importance to IV and DT. Their tension made the air feel tighter, as if any misplaced word could shift the entire investigation in a direction none of us wanted. Whenever one agent began to apply pressure, he was quickly replaced by another.

At no point was I restrained, though each agent made it clear that I would not be leaving until they had a clearer picture of the situation.

Those early rounds of questioning were interrupted only once, by a doctor who entered to examine me. He drew blood, collected a hair sample, and then left as abruptly as he'd arrived. The interrogation continued for hours, but nothing new emerged, only what I had already told them.

Eventually, I was escorted by a male and female agent to what could only be described as a lavish suite, located in the same building as the interrogation room. The contrast was jarring, the soft lighting and expensive furnishings creating an eerie stillness that felt nothing like freedom.

Who came into that suite, and what was discussed, I am not at liberty to disclose until there is a resolution. Normally, withholding facts would go against my nature, but for now, with BB and Serg still missing, I'll save those details for another time—in the interest of their safety. What I can say is that the minutes inside that suite felt heavier than anything that had come before, as if the walls themselves were waiting for answers none of us had.

For now, all I can do is start where the world first realized something was terribly wrong.

Chapter 4: Disappearing Acts

Here is what I can share. Some of it is fact, and much of it is speculation.

What the worldwide television audience expected to see — the trophy presentation — turned instead into confusion. As cameras panned across the disoriented crowd, perplexed announcers struggled to describe what was happening. The uncertainty grew exponentially as the broadcast continued. Spectators at the venue and viewers at home were equally bewildered, whispering and posting as the realization spread that something was terribly wrong.

Within minutes after the tournament ended, with excitement from the dramatic finish still hanging in the air, a switch seemed to flip — and near pandemonium followed. Rumors spread instantly. Within seconds of the first change in the spectators' demeanor, broadcasters began reporting that BB had disappeared. No details were available. Everyone was in disbelief. To most, it felt like an impossible magic trick, one that left the audience shaking their heads, wondering how it had been done.

Live feeds soon showed DT and IV entering the clubhouse, surrounded by a surge of men in suits, dark glasses, and headsets. The images transfixed millions of viewers across the world. As the crowd's confusion turned to panic, the growing presence of agents and officials filled the periphery of the country club until it barely resembled the place it had been moments earlier. Helicopters hovered above. Vehicles poured onto the grounds. Those who had remained for the trophy ceremony suddenly found themselves detained, unable to leave or even move about. Within minutes, automatic weapons appeared in the camera frames.

Gradually, as the world watched, order began to replace the chaos. Spectators at the country club were herded into small groups across the fairways by Secret Service agents, reinforced by others in riot gear. Cars lined up at the exits were halted. Every road surrounding the country club was shut down. Then, one by one, the live transmissions began to fade until the visuals stopped altogether. Yet the silence on screen only amplified the noise elsewhere. With no footage to show, broadcasters filled airtime with endless speculation. Newsrooms buzzed; anchors grasped for answers. Everyone knew something monumental had happened, but no one knew what.

Within an hour of the tournament's conclusion, nations worldwide were aware of the international incident unfolding in the United States. The celebrity granddaughter of one of the most powerful families on Earth had vanished. Not only BB, but also the grandson of the most powerful family in Russia, had disappeared. Governments everywhere recognized the sensitivity of the moment and the need to tread carefully as they considered how to respond to both the U.S. and Russia over such an explosive event.

By the second news cycle, unconfirmed details flooded the airwaves. Few wanted to use the word *abduction*, though many hinted at it. Early reports included photographs showing two individuals in red uniforms, zipped up the front, wearing matching red golf caps. They were seen leaving the entrance to the women's locker room only minutes after BB had entered the scorer's tent. The two — one man with short hair, one woman with flaming red hair — wore large-lensed sunglasses that concealed much of their faces. Each carried equipment cases, which they loaded onto the back of an official's golf cart before driving away from the building.

It was later determined that one of them handed a note to the Secret Service agent stationed outside that door. The couple leaving the clubhouse was misidentified as the cameraman and assistant assigned to film BB's post-tournament interview. Their exit route and destination were never discovered.

Hours after the detainment of everyone on site — spectators, staff, media crews, security teams, competitors, entourages, and the thousands of vehicles in the parking lot and surrounding streets — most had been searched, questioned, and slowly released. Local police manned roadblocks on every street within a ten-mile radius, inspecting every car for the missing pair.

Within twenty-four hours, every form of global media was reporting the same conclusion: the couple had vanished from the area without a trace, leaving behind only questions big enough to swallow the world's attention whole.

Chapter 5: The Making of BB

BB—known throughout the world of Trikers, is the name on everyone's lips across the United States and Russia. For six days now, hawks and doves alike have argued her fate. The hawks raise their rhetoric toward conflict, claiming our nation's treasure has been kidnapped, or worse. The more cautious voices, however, find hope in the fact that the two most powerful and, at times, aggressive leaders in the world have remained notably restrained, avoiding any escalation of this already volatile situation. That restraint has become its own fragile thread, one the entire world seems to be holding its breath over

For those unfamiliar with BB and Serg, here is the official information on their backgrounds, along with some personal insight from my own experience with them.

Our nation's most celebrated athlete — and a role model of the highest order — became a household name at the age of twelve. BB was both the architect and the face of *IE*, a school program that spread across the country like wildfire. Its mission: to reduce bullying and raise the sense of self-worth among students nationwide. What stood out most was her wisdom at such a young age, and the fact that since IE's introduction, participation in team-based IE programs has rivaled, and often surpassed, the popularity of traditional school sports. Even then, she carried herself with a strange mixture of confidence and humility, as if she understood the weight of her influence long before the rest of us did. Her boundaries were clear, even at thirteen, and she protected them with the kind of steadiness most adults never master.

My first introduction to BB came through an interview about the rapid success of her program. National statistics on bullying and youth mental health were showing measurable improvement, and team participation rates were soaring. Every news outlet and social media platform was buzzing with the story. The only interviews BB ever agreed to were those focused solely on IE — she would stop mid-sentence if anyone tried to veer into her personal life.

That first interview remains unforgettable. BB, still a young teenager, spoke with the composure and clarity of someone far older. She credited the many educators and students who had helped pilot the program in its early days, refusing to take credit for its success. In every conversation I've had with this remarkably engaging young woman, one quality always stands out: her passion for putting others first. *IE* was a concept born from collaboration, implemented through teamwork, and its success belonged as much to each school and student as it did to its creator. Talking to her never felt like speaking to a prodigy. It felt like speaking to someone who genuinely believed the world could be kinder and was determined to prove it.

Before *IE* made her an international name, BB was already well known because of her family, and her mesmerizing talent on the golf course. She wasn't just a golfer; she was one of the earliest and most skilled *Trikers*. Her athleticism, beauty, and lineage from a preeminent golfing family helped propel Trike Golf into global prominence.

Trike Golf, as its name suggests, combines traditional golf with the use of a trike. BB's custom trike, affectionately named *Butterfly*, would glide down lush fairways with a grace that captivated anyone who watched her play. The sport added a new physical and time-based dimension to the classic game, breathing life into a pastime that had seen a decade of decline. Golf courses around the world began adopting and promoting Trike Golf enthusiastically.

Competitive Trike Golf rounds finished in a quarter to a third of the time required for standard golf. That efficiency — combined with its fitness appeal — made it impossible for even the most traditional country clubs to ignore the increased rounds, revenue, and energy it brought.

"Trikers," as players came to be known, transformed golf's reputation from slow and methodical to fast and dynamic. They flowed across open fairways, sprinting toward greens and tees. For many, completion times became a greater point of pride than scores. And as a workout, few sports rivaled the intensity of Trike Golf.

BB's love for the sport was in her blood. From her grandfather down to herself, golf was the family's shared language. From a very early age, her extraordinary skill was apparent. Countless stories circulated about how her precocious talent often left her grandfather fuming, his pride in his own game repeatedly humbled by his young granddaughter's effortless victories. As she grew older and devoted herself to Trike Golf, her family began to acknowledge her unmatched ability and joined her in promoting both her career and this exciting evolution of the sport.

Before one of our interviews, BB confided that her greatest joy in playing had little to do with scores or times, those were the obsessions of her mother and grandfather. What she loved most was the escape: the vast, shimmering green fairways where she could finally feel alone, away from the relentless scrutiny that defined her life. She said the fairways felt like the only place big enough to hold her thoughts without crowding her.

She would spend entire days out there, adrenaline flowing, gliding from hole to hole, alone with her thoughts and dreams. Her Secret Service agents, ever-present and watchful, kept their distance, stationed discreetly in golf carts at the edge of her world. She told me she could play for hours and almost forget they were there. I remember the quiet longing in her voice when she said that — an ache for privacy that most of us take for granted.

For BB, golf wasn't just a sport. It was her sanctuary. Her safe haven. Her whole world shrunk down to a course and a club every time she'd pick up her golf equipment. I understood her in a way but at the same time, I had never felt so strongly about anything that I had in my life aside from her. A dream, a passion so intense that the rest of the world pales in comparison.

And maybe that was what kept her going amongst the white noise of her unwanted world. The love she held for her sport — her home — and everything that came with it.

Chapter 6: The Rise of Trike Golf

As the sport of Trike Golf has advanced in worldwide popularity, giving way to national and international tournaments, BB has become the face of this newest sports surge in the U.S. Many have compared its rise to the lightning-fast ascent of snowboarding from skiing, where today, there are likely more boarders on the slopes than skiers.

Competitive "Trikers" have taken Trike Golf to another level, with open courses before them, new tech elements added to balls and flags, and competition that pushes the game into another dimension. Sub-hour rounds are now the norm, even on some of the most arduous terrains to pedal.

Many traditional golf professionals rave about the changes Trikers have brought to the game, the most striking of which is the athleticism required to pedal at full speed while stopping to play a handful of shots on each hole. Many players new to the sport admit that the physical aspect is harder to master than the ball-striking skills.

BB is a player who makes every facet of the sport seem effortless. Her demeanor and rhythm have been described as that of a bird soaring through the sky, while her competitors describe her as a bird of prey — one few can match.

BB's incredible talent and her joy on the course became the impetus for her parents and grandfather to build tournaments that showcased their family's celebrity and expanded their golf-related brand. But there was a far more compelling motivation for BB. With the growth of Trike Golf and tournaments worldwide, she found an outlet to pursue her true passion; helping others.

She used her family's desire for her to perform and bring notoriety to their name as a means to create and expand her own interests. As a teenager, BB convinced her parents to loan her seed capital to buy a trike manufacturing company so she could design and create custom trikes.

The new company, now known as *Ali Inc.*, was an immediate success. In addition to producing trikes for both regular and competitive play, BB developed an entire line for a very different purpose. She meticulously scheduled her own events in which to compete, and it quickly became obvious — to both her family and the world — that the locations she chose were more about her desire to help others than about competition. These choices hinted at a quiet maturity she rarely showed at home, a steadiness that made her mission feel intentional rather than rebellious. It was a passion project that she nurtured herself, with love and care.

BB brought her family name and her company's products to places where she could identify those who would truly benefit from her specialized line of trikes. These "Model Ts" were created to be given, not sold, to those who needed them most. Each recipient also received lifetime access to her online shop for any follow-up needs to help maintain their equipment. Her generosity wasn't performative; it was methodical and personal, the kind of care that left people feeling seen.

As often as family members tried to dissuade BB from her philanthropic endeavors — arguing that it came at the cost of company profits — she would remind them that her business was successful the way she intended it to be, and that it was *her* company. Those reminders were gentle but firm, the quiet confidence of someone claiming her own path.

The fact that the only interviews she ever gave were those that expanded her mission and her passion for others became her hallmark. That consistency was a virtue recognized around the world. The less she said about herself, the more her name was admired.

It was through this same devotion to shining her light on others' needs that an interview was arranged shortly after her sixteenth birthday, and her first major tournament win. The timing felt symbolic, almost like a doorway opening into the life she was meant to shape for herself.

Chapter 7: The Secret Service Report

This statement is being submitted in the case of a missing person, most commonly known as BB. I am employed by the United States Secret Service, badge number 44825. On the day my charge went missing, I was assigned to her personal security detail and stationed inside the women's locker room of the clubhouse at the time of her disappearance. I offer this account with full acknowledgment that every decision I made that day carries weight, and that my responsibility was to protect her.

At that time, the principal, BB, had just won a major international Trike Golf tournament and had entered the women's locker room through the side door after completing her scoring in the scorer's tent. Minutes before her arrival, per her prearranged request, a journalist and his crew had been admitted to the main area to await her for a brief interview while tournament officials finalized the details of the awards ceremony. My service partner that day was stationed at the side door, responsible for authorizing entry and exit only to approved individuals. There was nothing unusual, nothing that suggested the next hour would change everything.

Immediately after entering, BB requested that I escort the journalist's two assistants — a cameraman and a female technician — to the main area. The cameraman was approximately 5'10" to 6 feet tall, weighing between 165 and 185 pounds, around twenty-four to twenty-eight years old, with dark brown hair mostly covered by a red golf cap bearing the tournament logo. He wore a one-piece light brown jumpsuit zipped up the front with the words "Tournament Official" stitched on the back, along with black canvas shoes and black socks.

The other assistant was a woman between 5'4" and 5'6", weighing approximately 110 to 130 pounds, with shoulder-length bright red hair also covered by a matching cap with the tournament logo. She wore an identical uniform and carried a mid-sized leather shoulder bag containing accessories for the interview. Her age appeared to be in her early twenties. Neither individual displayed any behavior that raised concern. Their demeanor was neutral, almost forgettable, which in hindsight has stayed with me more than I wish it did.

Less than a minute before the crew arrived, the journalist — of Russian descent — entered through the same side door. He was dressed casually in gray slacks with a black belt and a light blue dress shirt open at the collar. He wore oxblood-colored penny loafers and black socks, stood between 5'10" and 6 feet tall, and weighed approximately 160 to 180 pounds. His dark brown hair reached the top of his ears and collar. He carried a mid-sized legal pad and two pens branded with the country club logo. His confidence was noticeable, but not unusual for members of the press assigned to high-profile athletes.

The journalist introduced himself and stated that the champagne and glasses on the nearest table were placed there at BB's request, to celebrate both her tournament victory and her birthday. He offered to open the bottle and pour four glasses after I inspected it to confirm it was unopened. Upon clearance, he poured four glasses — one each for himself, his two assistants, and BB — preparing for a celebratory toast upon her arrival. There was a brief moment of levity, a softness in BB's smile when she saw the setup, that makes the events that followed even more difficult to recount.

Approximately two minutes and forty-two seconds after the assistants entered the main women's locker area, BB arrived. She asked that I allow her and the journalist a few minutes of privacy following the toast to discuss interview details, and that I escort the assistants into the locker and bathroom area off the main room in the meantime. I radioed this information to the agent at the front door, relaying BB's request for temporary privacy.

After the toast between BB, the journalist, and his assistants, I guided the assistants into the locker area and advanced a short distance into the adjoining bathroom, maintaining visual contact while giving them some space. As I waited for the signal to return them to the interview area, I heard a report through my earpiece that the assistants had already packed up and left in their assigned cart.

At that moment, I turned toward the two assistants within my line of sight and realized they were still seated on the locker benches, and unconscious. The sight stopped my breath. For a moment I couldn't process what I was seeing. Then training kicked in. I immediately moved toward the main room. A quick visual inspection confirmed that BB and the journalist were gone. I opened the exterior door and alerted the agent stationed outside. We exchanged details of the situation and broadcast across our communication network that the principal had disappeared.

We rechecked the women's locker room and began reviving and questioning the journalist's assistants. Both appeared confused but cooperative. Each claimed to have no memory beyond the toast and being escorted to the locker area. It was later confirmed that both had been recently hired for the interview: the cameraman at BB's personal request, and the female assistant through a local agency at the journalist's recommendation. Both appeared genuinely shocked and had no pertinent information. Their fear felt real. They seemed like casualties rather than participants.

While the locker room was being searched and the assistants questioned, we monitored communications for any reports of sightings or detentions of the missing pair. It became increasingly apparent that the situation was escalating. Every second without new intel felt heavier than the last.

Worse news followed — the cart, along with the brown uniforms and red caps, had been found abandoned between two parked vans in the parking lot. The scene outside was chaotic, with local law enforcement already securing all vehicles and preventing any departures. Federal and local agencies on-site quickly recognized the severity of the situation and began coordinating a full-scale search of the country club grounds. The shift from calm protocol to controlled panic was immediate and palpable.

By the time the principal's family members — her mother and grandfather — were escorted through the side door into the women's locker room, tension levels had reached their peak. Coordination among responding teams was fragmented, with multiple agencies attempting to assess known facts, probable dynamics, and immediate next steps.

When the family entered, emotions in the room erupted. Communication suffered, and the lack of answers only fueled confusion. I suggested relocating the response base to another part of the country club to improve coordination and establish a controlled command post. Determining the perimeter for containment was difficult, especially with thousands of spectators and staff still assuming that the commotion was related to the tournament rather than the disappearance, of which only a few were aware, and many of those were equally uncertain. The air felt thick with panic, even in the silence between radio calls.

The first ten to fifteen minutes passed without new intelligence. Meanwhile, the media, the crowd, and millions watching worldwide began to learn that BB was missing. The probability of immediate recovery was diminishing quickly. What should have been the brightest day of her career dissolved into uncertainty within minutes.

As much as family members wished to take control, it became clear that the situation required calm, professional coordination. When senior agents assigned to the family arrived, my role as lead agent concluded. After I briefed them on what my partner and I had observed, command transitioned to the senior team. I was reassigned to assist with coordination efforts being established in the country club's administrative offices and main conference hall. Stepping back felt like failing her, even though protocol demanded it.

Roadblocks were set up on all roads and paths within a twenty-mile radius of the club. Every vehicle was inspected before leaving the property and again before reaching its destination.

The most mystifying aspect remains how, in a matter of seconds, BB and the journalist vanished, leaving only an abandoned cart and two empty vans. Both vans were confirmed rentals, registered under the same tournament sponsor, who later admitted to renting only one.

As the search efforts continued, the urgency of the situation mounted, and all leads seemed to grow colder. Even the agents spoke in softer tones, as if the building itself could feel what we were afraid to say aloud. The mystery deepened, and the world outside continued to watch, unaware of the gravity of what had transpired within the walls of the country club. With every passing hour, the chances of finding BB and the journalist grew slimmer, and the question on everyone's mind was no longer *if* they would be found, but *how* — and what it would mean for those left behind.

Chapter 8: Unraveling the Mystery

Though my Secret Service badge number has been disclosed, I feel it's important to share further details about the principal. Sometimes, it's the smallest, most seemingly mundane fact that holds the key to solving a mystery. And this case has become the most compelling mystery of my life. It's been six days, and yet we've found nothing. The vans, the cart, the abandoned attire have been photographed, logged, and circulated through every agency we have. Numerous tips have come in, but nearly all have been either irrelevant or unhelpful. Each false lead feels like a door closing in front of me, another reminder of how quickly she slipped through my grasp.

One of the few clues that hasn't been dismissed entirely is the report from multiple witnesses who claim to have seen a small glider or aircraft in the vicinity. While that information is both intriguing and distracting, it's also inconclusive. No flight records have surfaced from that day that could link to unaccounted departures or arrivals. A small number of flights in the area have been traced, but nothing unusual has come up. The witnesses who reported the glider could not provide solid details, whether it was large enough to carry passengers, or which direction it was heading.

However, it was generally agreed upon that it appeared to be heading west from the Country Club. That clue, despite its vagueness, remains our best lead so far. And still, And still, the hours keep piling up. Still, we have nothing. The silence where answers should be has become unbearable. Still, thousands of law enforcement officers, as well as private citizens, are tirelessly searching.

Complicating matters further is the journalist's background. A Russian national, a celebrity in his own right, and a nephew of Vladimir Putin. As such, countless Russian detectives are involved in the search, with a singular focus on finding him — and by extension, BB. If it weren't for the desperate need to locate two missing persons, the presence of so many Russian agents on U.S. soil would be highly problematic. But for now, whatever it takes to find them. International tensions mean nothing compared to the urgency of bringing her home.

I've spent the past seven years as a Secret Service agent assigned to the protection detail of BB. I admit, as the years passed and especially as I became the lead agent, I began to feel something paternal toward her. I have two daughters of my own, both a year younger and a couple of years older than BB. I love my daughters more than anything, but BB is something different. I have never met anyone as exceptional as she is.

It has been an honor beyond my imagination to serve her, even though I never envisioned the responsibility would one day weigh so heavily on me. It's not that my own daughters lack intelligence or beauty, but BB is one of the world's most intelligent, charismatic, insightful, healthy, and beautiful woman, with a maturity far beyond her years. You can't spend years guarding someone like her without being changed by it. She had a way of making you believe in things again. Hope. Goodness. Possibility.

I became the primary agent on her detail two years ago, after working three-day shifts, followed by three days off, around the clock, unless additional security was needed for other events. Over time, BB herself requested that I become her primary overseer. So, these feelings go beyond professional duty. In many ways, I feel like I've failed her, because she vanished while I stood only feet away. That truth sits in my chest like a weight I can't shift. I replay every second of that day on a loop, searching for the moment I should have noticed something — anything.

The only comfort I take from the situation is that I'm inclined to believe BB planned this escape herself rather than being abducted.

Since she was sixteen, it's been common knowledge that there was something between her and the Russian. It was clearer to me than it was to her parents, though they knew of their mutual interest. Her parents, ever meticulous about who BB interacted with, didn't understand the full extent of her relationship with Serg, but they were aware.

BB, being as diligent and creative as she is, kept her emotional connections completely discreet. She regularly communicated with Serg — what she called him in her emails — though, as far as I know, their interactions were limited to a few highly secure interviews. He was one of the very few people she chose to engage with on a deeper level.

BB was unlike most teens. Despite the constant public attention, she never sought it out. She didn't care for the media's obsession with her life. Interviews, for BB, were a platform for others' causes — not her own. She never accepted an interview that was oriented toward exposing her personal life. Her message was always about expanding awareness of others' needs, never about her own fame. Even when family members suggested using interviews to boost her "brand recognition," BB was unwavering: "Not going to happen." It was a point of pride for her, and I shared that pride, quietly, as someone who saw how rarely the world produces people like her.

I'm fairly sure, and the labs are working tirelessly to confirm, that BB and Serg had a secret code allowing them to communicate under the radar of ordinary email exchanges. How they managed it doesn't surprise me; knowing BB, I'm often amazed at how well they were able to maintain such a discreet line of communication. I had access to the emails, yet it never occurred to me to investigate them more thoroughly. It wasn't part of my job description. BB's emails were harmless, and as long as they weren't harmful, I saw no reason to interfere. Now, that restraint haunts me. I wonder whether I should have read between the lines or sensed what she was setting in motion.

What I did notice was the frequency and duration of their communications, an intimacy that I couldn't ignore. Though it wasn't my place to delve into her private life, I could see just how close they had become. It was a bond that, while not part of my duty to control, was certainly something I couldn't help but observe. And now, looking back, it's clear that the disappearance — BB's disappearance — may have been her decision all along. That truth brings me both relief and devastation. Relief that she might be safe. Devastation that she felt she had to slip away without trusting any of us to help her.

Chapter 9: Empathy and Ambition

The one word that most accurately describes BB, beyond her brilliance, athletic prowess, and social celebrity, is empathy. Throughout my time assigned to protect her and her siblings, she has consistently shown more gracious consideration for others than I have ever witnessed. Many times, I have been taken aback by her thoughtfulness toward people — so often, in fact, that it became just another routine part of her daily decisions. It happened so often that I sometimes forgot how rare it truly was — how disarming it felt to watch someone so young instinctively lead with kindness in a world that demanded hardness from her at every turn. She was so adept at recognizing the needs of others that this virtue became the dominant feature of BB's character, an instinct she carried like breath.

Seven years ago, when I was first assigned to her detail, I was soon introduced to her *IE* program in schools. The premise of the program was to foster school teams, much like traditional sports teams, but focused on championing the importance of each student and the empathy needed to create a better school environment. Students could freely join teams that competed both as individuals and as teams, with the goal of fostering a sense of worth and importance for every student. I still remember the first time she explained it to me: legs swinging beneath a chair too high for her, voice steady with the kind of conviction most adults grow into only after life has humbled them. The program took off like wildfire, amplified by family support and connections, and is now more popular than traditional sports teams in most schools. The statistics on bullying, fighting, suicides, and other negative behaviors have drastically improved since BB's program was implemented — a program designed and executed by a twelve-year-old who believed that children deserved to feel seen.

Suffice it to say, I am even more in awe of that effort now, looking back, than I was when I first witnessed it. The success of *IE* is nothing short of miraculous, and BB has always taken it in stride. Similarly, her extraordinary skill on the golf course, which many admire, seems secondary to her. What stands out more than her golfing ability is how she uses that skill to help others. Though parts of her golf history are well known, I will share what I have learned from working closely with BB over the past several years, things I saw not as headlines but as moments. The quiet kind that change the way you look at a person.

Before my assignment, BB was already a phenom on her family's golf courses. Media reports had chronicled the frustration her grandfather experienced as he repeatedly lost to her, a young girl who consistently outplayed him. It was said that it took *months, if not years,* for him to accept her supremacy on the course. He eventually began creating tournaments to showcase her skills. BB was one of the first true enthusiasts of *Trike Golf*, the new version of the sport that combined traditional golf with the physicality of pedaling a trike golf cart.

Trike Golf introduced both time and score elements, making the game faster and more competitive. *Trikers*, as they became known, grew the sport even more quickly than snowboarding had grown out of skiing. BB didn't just adapt — she flourished. And watching her, you got the sense she wasn't chasing victory as much as she was chasing a feeling: the rush of movement, the control of her own direction, the whisper of freedom at her back.

By the time I joined her detail, BB was already a celebrity, often featured in the media for her mesmerizing performances as she floated down lush fairways on her customized trike, *Butterfly*. As a pre-teen, BB's family had already started branding and showcasing her incredible abilities on the golf course. Her passion, skill, health, and beauty helped fuel the rapid growth of a niche sport that is now part of every golf course in the world. And yet, behind every dazzling public moment, there were private ones — small, fleeting

— where she looked almost fragile in her quietness. I used to wonder if anyone else noticed.

Trike carts were initially accepted only on public courses, but as the realization set in that full rounds could be completed in a quarter of the time, and with no damage to the course, Trike Golf grew exponentially. Within a few years, it became more popular on many courses than traditional golf. BB was always at the forefront of pushing golf courses to accept Trikers. She knew how to persuade, but never through force. People listened because she made them feel like partners, not obstacles — a gift I watched her refine year after year.

BB's involvement went far beyond simply being a Triker, she convinced her family to finance her purchase of a custom trike manufacturing company. As the sport exploded, with more rounds played on trikes than on electric carts, her business became one of the most successful in the industry. At the age of thirteen, BB purchased the company, I was there in meetings where adults three times her age underestimated her, only to leave looking faintly stunned. She had a way of remaining calm even when the room wasn't, of speaking in a steady tone that hid how deeply she feared letting people down. She never admitted that fear aloud, but I saw it — in her posture, in the way her hands tightened around the hem of her shirt when conversations shifted toward profit over people..

Though it was always clear that BB's family contributed to her success, it was equally obvious that her primary goal was different from the family's commercial interests. BB's focus was always on using the success of her business to give back. Her company donated thousands of trikes worldwide, especially to those who could benefit most from them. Her company also created accessories for both Trikers and individuals who used the trikes for purposes beyond golf. Despite the regular pressure from her family to prioritize profits, BB remained firm. It wasn't rebellion. It was devotion — to strangers she'd never meet, to kids who needed hope, to anyone who reminded her of who she might have become without the safety of privilege. She carried that awareness heavily, even when no one else could see the weight.

The stories of BB's philanthropy — some known, many more not — were a major factor in her company's incredible success.

BB often shared that her passion for playing golf, especially on *Butterfly*, was driven by the freedom it offered her. On the course, she let herself be a teenager. She could breathe there — fully, deeply — in a way she rarely did in the presence of her family or the press. Watching her pedal away always felt slightly bittersweet: I wanted her to have that freedom, and yet every instinct in me tightened at the sight of her growing smaller in the distance. Protecting her meant letting her go, again and again.

In recent years, her family has increased their focus on creating major tournaments to showcase both the sport and BB's growing influence. And though BB would always compete, her primary motivation seemed to be the opportunity to use the sport's success to help more people. She was constantly seeking new ways to help, while those who managed her company were inspired by her dedication and worked alongside her to fulfill that mission. She was adamant that the company was *hers*, that she had repaid their investment, and that it would be run according to her values, not based on profit.

BB's company holds several patents for innovations that have dramatically influenced both Trike Golf's competitive side and the sport's overall success. The tournament that culminated in her incredible win — and eventual disappearance — was her fourth major tournament victory. Like professional golf, several international Trike Golf competitions have become major events, in no small part due to BB's family's involvement. The tournament held six days ago, on the final day of the three-day event, was especially significant — it was BB's eighteenth birthday.

But something in her had shifted that week. Something small, but unmistakable, like a thread pulled loose beneath a tapestry. Her smiles didn't reach her eyes as easily. Her silences stretched longer. And every time Serg's name came up, even indirectly, there was a flicker — relief, longing, something I didn't want to name. Looking back on it, it's easy to see that, in the week leading up to that tournament, it was clear to me that seeing Serg was more important to BB than winning, competing, or even celebrating her birthday.

And if I'm honest, even then… I felt the dread before I understood it.

Chapter 10: The Choice Made

The RV slowed as we entered the narrow road that ran between the fields like a forgotten seam. The morning light was thin and pale, barely touching the tops of the grass. Everything felt washed out, as if the world had not fully decided to wake up. It created the kind of quiet that made my chest tighten in a way that was not fear but something close to disbelief. The idea that we had made it this far felt like holding something delicate in my hands, afraid to squeeze too tight or drop it altogether.

Spiro was focused on the path ahead. His grip on the wheel stayed steady, but the tension in his shoulders told the truth. We were both running on the last bit of adrenaline we had. I kept glancing behind us, even though I knew no one was there. Old habits are stubborn. When you grow up watched, followed, guarded, and managed, it becomes normal to expect that someone is always close behind. Silence never feels like silence. It feels like a warning.

"We are close," he said. "Almost there."

His voice was low, calm, and even though I knew he was doing that for me, I felt like deep down, this quiet admission — reassurance — was just as much for him as it was for me. He had been steady throughout this entire thing, the calm center of something that could have spiraled apart at any second. I nodded, but my thoughts were anything but calm. They were pulling at me from every direction. Relief mixed with guilt. Fear mixed with hope. A strange kind of excitement that did not feel safe to trust. I kept thinking about the people who were already looking for me. The agents who had guarded me for years. My sisters. Even my mother, who would be furious and frightened at the same time. I felt the weight of their panic even though they were far from here. It pressed at me in a way that reminded me why leaving had been the only choice that would ever let me breathe.

The trees grew thicker as the road curved sharply. Branches brushed the RV, scraping the metal with a sound that made my pulse jump. I watched the shadows shift across the windshield and reminded myself that no one was out there. No team of agents. No watchers. Just wind and trees. It was strange to realize how hard it was to trust something so simple.

Then, through a break in the trees, the cabin came into view.

It looked the same as the last time we saw it. A small, weathered structure tucked far enough off the main road to be invisible from any direction unless you knew exactly where to look. It did not stand out. It did not shine. It did not scream importance. That was what made it perfect. For once, I wanted a place that did not announce who lived inside it.

Spiro parked beside the porch and turned off the engine. The sudden quiet felt heavier than the noise had. We sat there for a moment, neither of us moving. I could feel my heartbeat in my throat. My hands felt cold even though the morning was mild. Every step of this escape had been planned, but nothing in the planning prepared me for the moment when everything stopped and I had to face the life I chose over the life I left.

Spiro looked at me. "You ready?"

This time I did not answer right away. My mind moved through every version of myself I had been. The daughter. The granddaughter. The athlete. The public figure. The girl who had been protected so strictly that sometimes even her thoughts felt supervised. Then I thought about who I had been with him. More open. More honest. Less afraid to speak. Less afraid to want things. Less afraid to lose things. I was scared now, but the fear felt different. It felt real and alive, not imposed on me by someone else.

"Yes," I said. "I am ready."

We stepped out of the RV. The air smelled clean. Fresh pine, damp earth, something slightly sweet drifting from the fields. I breathed it in slowly, deeper than any breath I had taken in a long time. I waited to hear a radio crackle or the sound of tires on gravel or someone calling my name. Nothing happened. Just quiet. A real quiet, not the heavy kind that sat on you like a warning. This quiet felt like space.

Inside, the cabin was still and simple. One small room with a bed against the wall, a little kitchen area, a table with two chairs, and shelves with the supplies we had placed here weeks ago during one of our secret preparation days. It felt strange to see it all again. When we hid these things here, it felt like planting seeds for a life I was not sure I would ever be brave enough to claim. Now here I was. Standing inside the life I chose.

We moved around the room quietly, checking windows and locks. It was partly caution and partly a need to keep our hands busy because the weight of everything was trying to settle too quickly. I could feel myself trembling. My knees felt weak. My breath felt uneven. Not because I was doubting the choice, but because the reality of it was finally catching up to me. Running was one thing. Arriving was another.

I sat down on the edge of the bed because standing felt like too much. My hands shook, and I clasped them tightly so it would stop. Spiro noticed. He walked over and knelt in front of me, placing his hands gently around mine. The warmth grounded me in a way nothing else had.

"You did it," he said. "We are here."

"I am scared," I whispered. The words came out before I could stop them. I was not used to saying things like that out loud. My whole life had been about looking composed, looking prepared, looking steady. Being scared was allowed only in private, and even then, only if you got over it quickly.

"I know," he said. "So am I."

Hearing him say that softened something inside me. He had been strong through all of this, but not in a way that made me feel small. His strength was something that made sense beside mine. Not over it. Not around it. Beside it. I felt my eyes sting. I blinked hard, not wanting tears, but they came anyway. Not painful ones. Not the ones that come from stress or fear. These felt like pressure finally breaking.

He lifted my chin gently. "You do not have to hold yourself together here. Not with me."

That was all it took. Everything I had been holding in spilled over inside me. The fear of being caught. The guilt over leaving without a single word. The relief of finally taking control. The years of wanting him but never being allowed to touch him the way I wanted. The endless pressure of being someone the world watched but never truly saw. It all rushed through me, and instead of drowning in it, I felt it lift off piece by piece.

He leaned in and kissed me. It was not fast or urgent. It was lingering, slow, steady. It felt like a promise, but not the dramatic kind people write songs about. It felt like someone finally being allowed to touch something they had cared for quietly for years. I felt warmth spread through my chest. I felt my breath catch. I felt myself return the kiss with something that had been waiting far too long.

When we pulled back, our foreheads rested together. Neither of us spoke for several seconds. It was enough just to breathe in the same space without fear of who might be watching.

He took my hand again. "No more hiding."

I nodded. "No more codes. No more pretending we barely know each other."

He smiled a little. "No more living under someone else's plans."

We sat there together while the room settled around us. The morning light crept across the floor, slow and gentle. The cabin warmed a little. The quiet deepened. For the first time, I felt what freedom actually was. Not distance. Not secrecy. Not running. It was space to sit in a room and feel like all of you was allowed to exist there.

After a few minutes, he spoke again. "What now?"

The question hung between us. It was bigger than the room, bigger than the porch outside, bigger than the cabin itself. It was not about today. It was about everything that would come after.

I looked around the room. At the bed. At the small table. At the window that looked out into the trees. None of it was fancy. None of it was part of the world I had known. Yet all of it felt more honest than any place I had ever been.

"Now we learn who we are without all the eyes on us," I said. "Now we build something that belongs to us, not to everyone else."

He nodded, and I saw the same relief in his eyes that I felt in my chest. This was not escape anymore. This was life.

We unpacked slowly. We talked quietly. We moved around each other with a kind of soft awareness that came from finally being allowed to be close. Every step felt new even though we had known each other for years. Every small task felt like a tiny act of building something that no one else could claim.

As the hours passed, the world outside grew brighter. Birds moved through the trees. The wind softened. The day settled into itself. And through it all, we stayed inside our little cabin, steady in a way that felt new and fragile and strong all at once.

By late afternoon, the shadows stretched long across the floor. I stood at the window and looked out at the road, half expecting to see something or someone appear. But nothing moved except the breeze.

"They will look for you," Spiro said from behind me.

"I know."

"They will search every possibility. Every road. Every border."

"I know."

"You chose this anyway."

I turned to him. "Because I would not survive the life I left."

He crossed the room and wrapped his arms around me. I rested my forehead on his shoulder. His heartbeat was steady. Mine began to match it. The simple act of standing there in silence with him felt like more freedom than I had ever imagined.

"This is our life now," he said.

"Yes," I said. "It is."

And it was. Not because the world allowed it, but because we stepped into it ourselves.

The search would continue. The theories would grow. My family would rage. Governments would scramble. The world would talk because they needed a story that made sense to them.

But none of that touched us here.

We had made our choice.

And for the first time in my life, my choice was enough.